HARRON LEE

THE RELUCTANT
OUTDOORSMAN

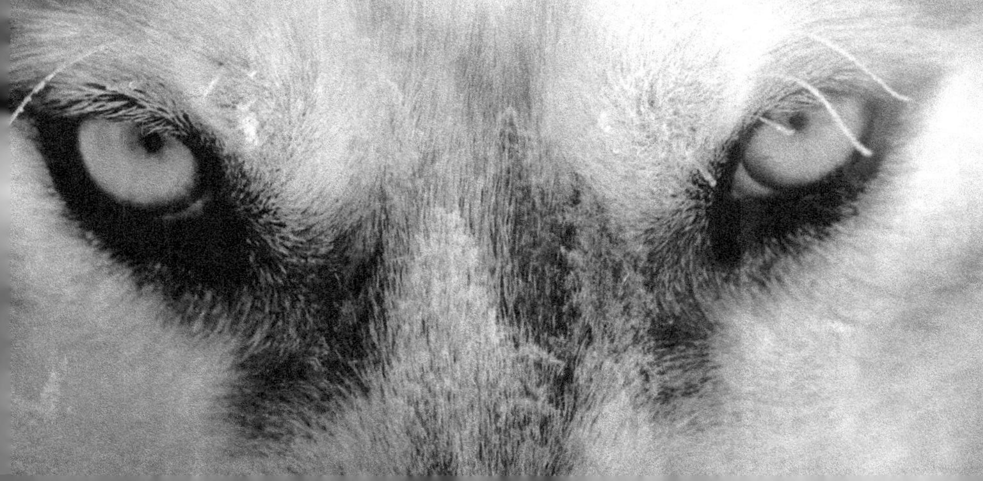

WORKBOOK PRESS LLC
187 E Warm Springs Rd,
Suite B285, Las Vegas, NV 89119, USA

Website: https://workbookpress.com/
Hotline: 1-888-818-4856
Email: admin@workbookpress.com

Ordering Information:
Quantity sales. Special discounts are available on quantity purchases by corporations, associations, and others.
For details, contact the publisher at the address above.

ISBN-13:   978-1-958176-79-5 (Paperback Version)

REV. DATE: 06/21/2022

Chapter 1

"What are you doing for your holiday, Peter? My family is going to Walt Disney World for two weeks. I can't wait," Jimmy said loudly trying to be heard over the noise that surrounded them. They weaved between students saying goodbye to their friends for the summer, students shutting lockers for the last time that school year, and students stuffing their backpacks with all their locker contents. Excitement filled the air now that summer vacation had officially started.

"I wished I was doing that," Peter said gloomily. "I will be going fishing with my father," Peter said as he bit his bottom lip nervously.

"That sounds like fun. What is the problem?" Jimmy asked as they joined the students that spewed out of the school's large front doors onto the paved sidewalk which lead to the street.

"My father was so excited about taking me fishing this summer. I didn't want to disappoint him so I agreed to go but now I am having second thoughts," Jimmy said as he screwed up his face and bit the side of his lip. "You know that he lives in the Yukon. He is always telling me about seeing different animals when he is out in the woods. I don't know anything about his world except what he tells me. How can I make him proud of me? I don't know what to do if I met a bear," Peter said with panic in his voice. "He wants me to walk a couple of miles to one of his favorite fishing holes in Algonquin Park. The longest walk I have done was following my mother through the mall on one of her shopping sprees. That exhausted me and I wasn't carrying a full backpack at the time. How am I going to live up to his expectations?"

"Can you back out saying you are sick or something?" Jimmy asked.

"Nah, he is picking me up in a few hours.   I have been reading about surviving outdoors and different animals but it is not the same as actually being in the woods. I am so nervous about it that I have hardly been sleeping. I can't back out. It would break my father's heart."

"That is tough."

"My mother isn't helping matters either."

"What is she doing?"

"She is insisting that I take everything but the kitchen sink with me. I can't carry everything she wants me to take."

"What does your stepfather say about this?" asked Jimmy.

"I didn't really tell him of my fears. I just said that I hoped I wouldn't be the world's worst outdoorsman. He said even if I was my father would love me anyway. He doesn't know that my father thinks that living in the city is turning me into a marshmallow."

"Well, you do have the shape of a marshmallow," Jimmy said with a smile on his face.

"Thanks, you aren't too skinny yourself," Peter said as he reached for the handle to their apartment building's door.

"Hope everything goes all right for you, Peter," Jimmy said as he headed down the left hall.

"Have a good time at Disney World," Peter called out as he headed into the elevator and pushed the eleventh floor button as the doors shut in front of him. He was surprised when the doors opened to reveal his mother standing there.

"Where have you been? Your father called. He is going to be here in an hour and a half. Hurry we have to get you fed," she said as she hustled him down the hall to their apartment.

Peter headed to his room to put his school bag away before he washed up for dinner. When he opened his bedroom door, he stopped dead and cried out "Mom!"

"What?" she called from the kitchen.

On his bed laid a huge suitcase and his backpack. Both were stuffed to their limit. "I can't take all this with me. How am I going to drag all this through the woods?" Peter cried out.

"I just packed the things you will need," his mother said as she walked toward his room drying her hands on a dish towel.

"Mom, I told you. I have to carry everything I take on my back. We are hiking into the woods. I can't lift my backpack," Peter whined as he struggled to lift it. "How am I supposed to get this suitcase through the woods?"

George, Peter's stepfather, came down the hall, "What is all the noise about?"

"Look at what mother wants me to carry through the woods," Peter wailed as he pulled his stepfather into his room.

"You need everything I packed. I was just trying to take care of you," Peter's mother said angrily as she turned and stomped back into the kitchen.

"Your mother loves you, Peter. She just wants to make sure you are warm and safe. She knows deep down your father will take care of you but to her the forest is a cold, scary place.

I guess I do too thought Peter as he opened his backpack

"It is hard to believe that she once lived in the Yukon with your father," commented George as he shook his head. "Didn't your father send you a list of what to bring?"

"Yes," Peter said as he grabbed the list off his desk.

"Pack the things your father told you to bring. He knows what you will need better than your mother or I do," George said.

Peter smiled at George. He felt like he was more like George than his own father. They both loved reading books and playing video games together. "I just hope I won't disappoint my father."

"You will be fine. Besides you are a reader so you can always draw on the knowledge you have learned from books." George said as he squeezed the boy's right shoulder. "When you are done, you better make up with your mother before you go."

Fifteen minutes later, they found Peter's mother in the kitchen stirring the spaghetti sauce.

"Mom, I am sorry. I know you were just trying to help," Peter said as he gave her a big hug.

"I just don't understand why anyone thinks sleeping on the ground with wild animals running around is fun. I will have your father's head if you get hurt or sick."

"Marianne, Peter will be fine. He is a smart ten year old."

"I guess," his mother said reluctantly. "Oh, Peter, you have to take this with you." She grabbed the spray can that was sitting on the counter and shoved it at him.

"What is it," Peter said as he took it from her.

"Bear spray. You have to take that with you or you are not going," his mother insisted as she hugged him so hard he could hardly breathe.

George winked at Peter and said, "You better let him go or he won't have time to eat before he goes."

"Oh, yes…sit down. I will get your spaghetti."

Chapter 2

The doorbell rang at 5:55 p.m. Peter hurried out of his bedroom carrying his coat over his arm and his backpack over one shoulder. His stomach felt like a thousand butterflies were fluttering around inside him. He was excited to see his father but scared all at the same time about this trip.

George answered the door. "Hi, Butch, how are you doing?" He extended his hand.

Butch shook his hand as he stepped into the apartment. "Hi George, where is my boy?"

"Right here, Dad," Peter said as he peeked out from behind the closet door where he was looking for his boots. "I am almost ready to go."

"Hold on, Buddy. I have to talk to your mother and stepfather first."

"Ok, I will get my boots on you sent me," Peter said as he pulled them out of the closet and started pulling them on. He had been walking the halls of the apartment building every evening to get them broke in for hiking like his father had suggested.

Butch followed George into the living room where Marianne sat fretting about letting Peter go on the trip with hardly any warm clothes.

"Hi Marianne, how are you?"

"Upset, I shouldn't have agreed to this trip."

"All we are doing is going fishing," Peter's father said.

"Yes in the woods with wild animals."

"Animals usually run away from humans. There is nothing to worry about," said Butch.

"Now Marianne, you have already agreed to the trip so you can't back out now. Peter is looking forward to it," George added.

"Ok, Ok, but I have something for you," Marianne said as she disappeared into the kitchen. She returned carrying a large insulated bag.

"What is this," asked Butch as she handed it to him.

"Food, Peter is a growing boy. He needs his full allowance of vitamins and minerals to stay healthy and strong."

"We can't carry that with us. I have dehydrated food packs and I can collect food as we hike to the river then we will be eating the fish we catch."

"But what if…," stuttered Marianne?

I know what I will be eating for the next week," George spoke up trying to diffuse the situation as he rifled through the bag.

"We will be in Algonquin Park for one week. The rangers will know the waterfall that we will be at. My phone does not work up there but I will call you as soon as I have service again."

"You better take good care of him," Marianne said sternly as she wagged her finger at Butch.

"Honey, Butch would not let anything happen to Peter if he could prevent it," said George as he put his arm around her shoulders and squeezed her.

"We better get going. I would like to get halfway there tonight. Let's get going Peter," Butch said as he entered the hall.

Peter gave his mother and stepfather a hug and kiss before he followed his father out of the door. "Bye, see you later," he called as he walked down the hall feeling anxiety. He wondered if he would see them later or would a wild animal have him for dinner.

CHAPTER 3

Butch drove his Jeep into the ranger's station parking lot the next morning. "Can you get the gear out of the back of the Jeep while I inform the rangers where we will be fishing?" Butch said as he undid his seat belt and climbed out of the vehicle.

"Sure, Dad," Peter said as he undid his belt and scrambled out of the Jeep. This is it he thought. There is no turning back now. Can I make my father proud of me? He pulled the backpacks from the Jeep and was just about to close the back door when his father reappeared. "I have everything ready to go," Peter said as he picked up his pack.

"You forgot something," his father said as he reached in and pulled out a bow and a quiver of arrows.

"Are we going to hunt animals?" Peter hesitantly asked not sure he wanted to kill any animal. The thought of that made him feel a little sick to his stomach.

"No, but I thought you would like to learn how to shot a bow and arrow so you can brag to your friends about your skill," Butch said with a smile on his face and a twinkle in his eyes.

"I would," Peter said excitedly. He knew his friends would be so envious of him when he tells them.

"Let's get going," his father said as he tied the bow and quiver to the side of his backpack. He then swung the pack gracefully onto his back.

Peter tried to copy the way his father put his pack on but all he succeeded in doing was to get his straps tangled. His father helped him straighten them and tighten them so the pack was sitting comfortably on his back. Peter felt stupid in front of his father. His father's words rang out in his head. Always check your gear before you leave and make sure everything is in good shape. His father believed that this practice had saved his life many of times. He should have had the straps set up before he left home but he had never taken the time to try it on.

Peter jammed his red ball cap onto his head and put his sunglasses on that his mother insisted he wear. He was even more determined to show his father that he could survive in the outdoors now.

His father led Peter to a wide path that lead into the woods. As they walked, they passed maples, alders, poplars, birches, spruces and pines. He almost fell backward as he looked upward trying to see the top of a pine tree that grew beside the path. They were the tallest trees that Peter had ever seen. As they walked along he began to notice a green fuzzy growth on the tree trunks and strange shaped vegetation growing out of the trees.

"What are those things on the trees, father?" Peter said as he pointed to several different growths on nearby trees.

"Those growths are different mosses, funguses, and mushrooms. They live off the trees."

"Oh," Peter said not knowing exactly what those plants were. He just knew that those mushrooms didn't look anything like the mushrooms he helped his mother cut up for her chilli recipe.

As they walked deeper into the woods, the smell of damp earth and rotting trees began to surround them. The rays of the sun dance on the path as the tree leaves rustled in the wind above their heads. The quietness of nature surrounded them. Peter was use to the noise of people on the busy streets of Toronto. This quietness sent a shiver down his spine as he continued to follow his father deeper into the woods. He felt scared and full of dread. Why he wondered? He knew his father would protect him.

The path began to narrow. The smell of rotting vegetation grew stronger with every step as well as the silence. Peter felt more and more uneasy as he realized he had no idea where he was. Everything looked the same.

Suddenly, a coo-ooo-woo rang out breaking this silence.

"What is that?" Peter jumped as he cried out.

"It is a mourning dove. See him just above your head on the third branch. He was just warning you to stay away from his nest. Do you see him?"

"How do you know it is a male bird?"

"His colouring and markings tell me what sex he is?"

"Why is he standing with his one wing out like that? Is it broken?"

"They like to sunbath so they pick trees to nest in that allow a lot of light to get through their branches. Then they build their nests so they can sunbath while they watch their nests."

"Smart birds"

"I bet if we looked into that nest we would find two eggs or hatchlings."

"How come you know so much about mourning doves," asked Peter.

"When I was a boy instead of playing games or watching television, I spent my time outside watching the animals that lived around my house."

"I read lots of books about different animals," Peter replied.

"Reading is all right but seeing the real animals in their own habitat is much better. I want to show you the wonderful world I live in with beauty everywhere you look. Not the cement and brick world, your mother has you living in."

"It is not that bad living in the city."

"It is to me," his father said as he put his arm around his son's shoulders as they continued down the path. "I hated working in an office every day and not being out in nature."

"When did you work in an office?" asked Peter.

"You were about a year old when I did. I wasn't happy then."

Peter stumbled over a root that stuck out of the ground.

His father caught him. "You have to watch where you are stepping. The roots of these trees can't grow downward because of the rocky ground. Instead they grow sideways weaving their roots into their neighboring tree roots so they can cling to this rocky hillside. That is also the reason that you see bends in some of the trees. As they were pushing up threw the ground they met rocks so they twisted or bent to move around the rock to reach the sunlight."

The trail began to climb upward. The trees were growing closer together, each fighting to reach the sunlight above. The canopy of branches over their heads became to thicken blocking out more of the sun until eventually they were walking in a shadowy quiet darkened world.

As they went his father pointed out robins, wrens, blue jays, and other birds that watched from the trees as they passed. He showed Peter tracks from different animals like the little hand like prints of the raccoon, and the doglike paw print of the fox. They even saw a doe with two fawns grazing near a small stream. They saw squirrels scurrying from tree to tree. They flushed out a few rabbits as they pushed bushes away so they could pass. Chipmunks sat chattering at them from the branches overhead.

The path began to get steeper as they climbed upward. It didn't take long before Peter started to get tired. He wished his father would take a break but he was determined he was not going to ask for one. Keeping up with his father was becoming more and more of a challenge with every step. His breathing was rapid and his legs felt like he had one hundred pound weighs tied to them. He struggled to keep up with his father who didn't seem to be bothered by the incline. Peter's one fear was to be left in this maze of trees alone.

He had no idea how his father knew where he was going. All the trees looked the same to Peter. His father didn't even glance at his compass very often as he led Peter deeper and deeper into the woods. When his father turned onto a very narrow trail leading deeper into thicker trees, they had to push branches out of the way as they moved forward. Twenty minutes later, they stepped into a clearing which seemed to hang out over the valley below.

"We will eat lunch here. I always like to spend time at this look out. It is so beautiful," his father said as he unbuckled his pack and dropped it on the ground.

"It is beautiful," Peter said as he looked out at mountains covered in trees and a river of sparkling water running through the trees below them. No wonder his father liked nature when you see such beauty every day, Peter thought as he took off his pack. He sank to the ground exhausted as he marvelled at a fluffy white cloud that looked like a horse with a rider as it moved over the mountains in the distance.

His father pulled out some beef jerky, dried fruits, and nuts for them to eat. They drank the water from their canteens. As they ate, they talked.

"You haven't told me how you did at school. Did you pass?"

"Yeah, I got four A's, the rest B's, except a C in history. I just can't seem to remember dates and names."

"You come by that naturally. That was the subject I used to hate," his father said as he shook his head and chuckled.

"You did?" Peter said. "Now I don't feel so bad about sucking at history."

"I still expect you to do your best at it, son." Butch said seriously.

"Did I tell you what happened to Jimmy?" Peter said.

"No, did he start another food fight in the cafeteria again. I sometimes wonder if he is a good influence on you."

"He only threw the food into Ralph's face to blind him so he could get away. Ralph ducked and some of the food hit some other people and suddenly someone yelled out food fight and everyone started throwing food. Ralph came after Jimmy a few days later and he put Jimmy in his locker. He was stuck......."

"Shhh...," his father said as he held up his finger to his mouth. His father crawled to the ledge and looked over it. He waved for Peter to move up beside him which Peter did quietly. When Peter looked over the ledge, he saw forty feet below them, a mother black bear and two cubs.

"The mother is showing her cubs how to hunt for ants, grubs, and other insects by overturning logs and stones," his father whispered into Peter's ear. "Sit quietly and watch them."

Peter almost laughed out loud when a stone a cub was trying to turn over flipped suddenly sending the cub tumbling backwards. They watched as the bears slowly moved farther and farther away until they disappeared into a clump of trees to the east of them.

"Wow, the guys won't believe that I was that close to a real black bear and her cubs out here. How did you know they were there?"

"You have to listen all the time for danger. The wind was blowing away from her so the bear didn't know we were here. Her eyes are not the greatest but her nose is fantastic. If we had walked into that mother bear, she would have sent her cubs up a tree. She could have attacked us if we had done anything that she interpreted as a threat to her babies."

"I have this," Peter said as he pulled out the can of bear spray from his pack."

Butch laughed, "I bet your mother made you bring that."

"Yes. Why? What is so funny?"

"A bear caused our marriage to break up."

"How did a bear do that?" Peter asked with surprise in his voice. He had always thought he was the cause of their breakup. One of his earliest memories was them fighting about whether he needed a coat to go for a walk with his father in the park. Shortly after that his father moved out of their apartment and he only got to see his father occasionally after that. Peter had always secretly blamed himself for their marriage breakup.

"At the time, we lived in the Yukon. I went to work one day and when I got home, you and your mother were gone. A bear smelled the apple pies that your mother was baking and decided he wanted some. She had the front door open to let a breeze in so the bear came in. She grabbed you and climbed out the bedroom window. She never went back to that house. She wanted me to give up my work and move to the city with her. She wanted no part of nature from then on. We moved to Toronto and I got an office job. I hated it. I tried but I was so unhappy. All we did was fight. The hardest thing I ever did was to give you up but city life was killing me slowly," his father said sadly.

"I never heard that story before that is why she is so panicky." Peter said as he realized that he hadn't destroyed their marriage. If felt like a weight had gone off his shoulders even though he hadn't thought about their break up for years.

"Yes. Now I live for my vacations with you and when we can talk on the computer."

"I know you love me, Dad, and I enjoy those times also."

His father gave Peter a squeeze. "Well, we better get going if we want to get our camp set up before dark."

"Ok," Peter said as he glanced at his watch which said one o'clock. How far where they hiking if his father was worried about darkness setting in before they got there? Peter began to worry. Will I be able to walk that far? He trudged behind his father who led them into an even thicker stand of trees. Moss and mushrooms grew among the tree roots and out of the fallen logs that were across their path. They had to climb under and over several fallen trees as they continued on. The smell of mold and rotting wood was intense. A small trickle of water ran over some nearby rocks as it headed downward toward the river below.

"Look, Dad, that mushroom is red with white spots. You always see them in colouring books and stories with elves but I didn't know they were real. Do you think elves really set under them like in children's books?"

"Maybe, but I have never seen an elf," his father said with a smile.

Tap, tap, tap rang out from nearby.

"Is someone building around here? Peter asked as he looked around for any sign of civilization.

"No, take your backpack off and follow me. I will show you the noise maker." They dropped their packs and his father led him into the undergrowth. They climbed over fallen trees and over large rocks. The sound of tapping got louder. His father stopped and pointed upward. Peter saw a white and grey bird with a bright red head hitting the old tree with its beak. "He is looking for insects. When he finds them, he uses his sticky tongue to catch them."

"I would have a major headache if I did that with my head. Look how fast he is moving."

"That is how woodpeckers get their food and make their nests for their young. You do not see many woodpeckers around anymore because humans are destroying their habitats. They need old trees for food and shelter but men are clearing more land, creosoting telephone poles, and stripping the land of dead trees."

"Can we do anything to help them?"

"Not unless you can teach men to live with nature instead of covering the land with cement and buildings."

This bothered Peter as he followed his father back to their gear. He wondered what he could do. He realized that he was enjoying the beauty around him and learning about nature.

CHAPTER 4

They had been walking for about an hour when Butch suddenly stopped and knelt down looking intently at something in the dirt. Peter was so tired he didn't notice and walked right into his father.

"Oh sorry," Peter muttered. All he wanted to do was to lie down and rest.

"Look at the wolf track. He is injured." His father looked around the area with a worried look on his face.

"How do you know that?" Peter said staring at the print over his father's shoulder. He could tell that his father was worried and he didn't understand exactly why.

"Look closely and see if you see a difference between the two front paw prints?" While Peter examined the prints his father got up and walked in a large circle around them.

"One is deeper than the other," Peter said after he looked at the prints for a few minutes. "Is his left foot twisted slightly?"

"Very good. It looks like the wolf had a broken leg and it didn't heal properly so he favors it. That could mean trouble. He may be hungry. There are no other wolf prints around here. That means he is a loner and not able to hunt bigger animals."

"We…eh…aren't considered food for wolves are we?" Peter said anxiously.

"Usually they avoid people, but when they are hungry a wolf will do anything for food especially if they smell blood."

"Oh, we are ok then aren't we?" said Peter as he looked around at the nearby trees nervously.

"Just to be on the safe side since that track isn't that old," his father said as he untied the bow and put an arrow in place as he led Peter down the path. Peter grabbed onto his father's backpack and held on tightly afraid of what they may encounter.

"How do you know that the track isn't that old?" Peter said in a low voice not wanting the wolf to hear them.

"Did you see the pile of poop that was a few feet away from the prints?"

"No,"

"Well, it was fresh and it was wolf poop."

"Oh," Peter said as he moved even closer to his father.

They continued along the trail but now his father stopped and showed Peter any tracks he found. There were deer, rabbits, skunk, and porcupine tracks. They even came across a turtle which was slowly crossing the trail. They didn't see any more wolf tracks which made Peter feel better. He hoped the wolf had found a meal and was heading in a different direction than they were.

They eventually started hearing the sound of splashing, gurgling water. With every step the sound got louder until they stepped into a small clearing on the shore of a pond. Fifty feet away, water cascaded over a fifteen foot cliff. To the right, the pond emptied into a swift moving river that disappeared into the woods some distance away.

This is my favorite fishing hole, his father announced as he turned in a circle taking in the beauty that surrounded them. "We need to get our camp setup and dinner started before dark," his father said as he dropped his backpack on the ground.

"We have hours before it gets dark," Peter said as he glanced at his watch.

"Not here, we are on the east side of this mountain so the sun sets when it goes behind that mountain to the west of us," his father said as he pointed toward a mountain in the near distance.

"Oh," Peter said as he saw how close the sun was to the top of the mountain.

"Put the tent up between those trees while I get some firewood," his father said as he untied a bag from the top of his backpack. He gave the bag to Peter and said, "If you see any sign of the wolf, climb that tree as high as you can go. I won't be long."

"Ok," Peter said as he took the bag and untied the knot that held it shut. All he wanted to do was to lie down and rest. Not wanting to show his father how tired he was, he bent over the bag and started taking poles, ropes, stakes, and the canvas tent out of the bag. He watched his father disappear into the woods. As soon as his father disappeared, Peter sank to the ground exhausted. He lay there several minutes before he decided that he better get going on the tent if he was going to impress his father. The problem was he had never put a tent together before. He had no idea how to fit all these pieces together to make a shelter. He sat there trying to see what pipes fit together all the while watching for wild animals. He didn't know what he would do if he saw one because he was too tired to run or climb a tree. Every sound and movement of the trees spooked him. All he could think of was the wolf slinking out from behind a bush and attacking him. He was so relieved when he saw his father coming out of the woods with an armful of wood.

His father immediately realized that Peter had no idea how to set a tent up when he saw all the pipes and canvas sitting in disarray. "Peter, hasn't your mother and stepfather ever taken you camping before?"

"Er…no, George isn't much of a sportsman and mom well you know what she thinks of sleeping outdoors," Peter stammered.

"When I was your age, I was learning how to track and hunt all kinds of animals including bear. I don't know what your mother ever saw in George. I bet his idea of roughing it is taking a walk in the park."

Peter giggled at that remark because it was true. Peter had never seen George do anything that would be considered roughing it. Peter also knew that his father didn't consider a man much of a man if he didn't hunt and fish.

"Let's get this tent up," his father said as he started fitting pipes together and shoving them in material pockets that stretched the canvas out to form a tent. He anchored the tent down with roped tied to stakes he pounded into the ground.

He then showed Peter how to start a fire which he put out immediately. He handed Peter the flint and his knife and said, "Your turn to try. You need to know how to make a fire to survive in the outdoors."

Peter took the dried leaves and fuzzy fibers his father had put out beside the circle of stones his father had designated as the camp fire. He put them in the middle of the circle and started striking the knife against the piece of flint. Sparks flew in all directions but not where he wanted them to go. Peter tried and tried until finally some sparks landed on the dried vegetation and started to smolder. He gently blew on it like his father had done until it burst into a small flame. Peter took the small twigs and more dried leaves and fed the flame slowly until it was burning brightly. He then started adding bigger pieces of wood until he had a nice fire burning.

"Dad, Dad, I did it! It took me awhile but I did it," Peter sat on his heels admiring the fire burning in front of him. "What was the fuzzy stuff you gave me to start it?"

"That is cattails. I collect them when I see them and pull the heads apart and dry them. You learn fast. Now it is time to make dinner." His father took a small Ziploc bag from his backpack. It had dried vegetables and dried meat in it. He also took out the mushrooms and wild carrots he had picked on the way there. "Can you get this pot full of water for me?"

"Sure, I will be right back," Peter said still glowing from the praise his father had given him. Peter knelt down at the water's edge and just dipped the pot in the water when a fish jumped a few feet away from him. Peter was so startled he dropped the pot and scrambled backwards from the water's edge.

"What is taking you so long," his father called.

"I was…watching the fish jump," Peter called back not wanting his father to know how badly the fish had scared him. With his heart still racing, he grabbed the pot and filled it with the cold water.

When he got back to the campfire, his father had built a pot holder over the fire. His father poured some of the water in the coffee pot which he put on a hot rock on the edge of the fire. The rest he left in the pot and hung it by its wire handle on the cross bar of his pot holder. Once the water was boiling, he added the ingredients from the plastic bag and stirred it. He then cleaned and cut up mushrooms and wild carrots he had found and added them to the pot. The mixture bubbled away. It didn't take long for it to turn into a thick stew.

His father then took a flat rock and positioned it near the fire to heat up.

He then mixed flour and water to make dough. He added the sugar and yeast mixture he had made earlier. He kneaded the dough and then took small pieces of it and flattened it on the heated rock. It rose into elliptical shaped and the collapsed into flat bread as it cooked quickly. His father dished out a bowl of stew and took the hot bread off the heated rock. He handed them to Peter. The delicious aroma made Peter's stomach growled loudly. His mouth began to water as he took the first spoonful of stew and then bit into the warm bread. He had never tasted anything that tasted so good before. It wasn't long before Peter was asking for seconds.

The sun disappeared behind the mountain and darkness began to surround them while they were still eating. The flames from the fire crackled and sparked as the smoke rose into the night sky. His father got up and went to a nearby tree. He broke off some sticks and they roasted marshmallows that he put on graham crackers and chocolate. He gave one to Peter to eat and had one himself.

"These are good. What is this called?" Peter said with chocolate and marshmallow smeared around his mouth.

"You mean you have never had smores' before."

"No, can I have another one." Peter said as he tried to lick the chocolate off his fingers.

"Sure you can," his father said with a smile. "Your mother is depriving you. I am going to have a talk with her," his father said as he put together another smores and handed it to Peter. Peter gobbled the treat down as they talked about their plans for the next day. A wolf howled nearby. Peter jumped dropping his last piece of smore on the ground.

"What was that?" Peter said anxiously looking around them.

"It is a wolf telling his pack where he is or that it is time to start hunting.

We have a few jobs to do before we go to sleep."

"What jobs?"

"We have to protect our food from thieves?" his father said as he pulled a cloth bag of food stuffs from his pack and a long thin yellow rope. He added the left over chocolate, graham crackers, and marshmallows to the contents of the bag and stood up. "Let's go."

"Who is going to steal our food out here?" Peter asked as he got up wondering where they were going. "There is no one else in the area is there?"

"It isn't human thieves I am talking about. All animals will steal our food if given the chance but raccoons are the worse. They are the safecrackers of the animal world. They have paws like little hands that are extremely sensitive. They can untie knots and open latches with them. They will do anything for a free meal."

"I read that they always wash their food."

"In captivity they do. The experts wonder if they are just washing the scent of humans off the food they are given."

"What about when they are in the wilderness?"

"They are mainly nocturnal and are rarely seen by people at night. They rarely are seen during the day unless food is scarce. So no one really knows if they wash their food all the time."

"What do they eat?"

"In the suburbs, they eat trash. In the wilderness, they like fish and eggs. They are not the only thieves in the area. Bears and wolves love an easy meal. That lone wolf would love a free meal and that call was close so we have to protect our food and ourselves."

"How do you protect the food out here?"

"We hang it up in the air where the animals can't reach it away from camp so they don't come near us."

His father chose a tall tree about one hundred feet from the camp. He tied a rock to one end of the rope and the sack on the other end. He threw the rock over a high branch. The rock landed on the ground nearby lifting the sack high in the air. He took the rock off the rope and tied that end to a nearby tree using several different knots.

"Can't the raccoons climb the rope?"

"No, they can't hold onto the rope. Their thumbs don't move like ours do."

"How do they climb on trees then?" asked Peter.

"They use their claws like hooks in the tree bark. They climb down head first by turning their back paws around and hooking their claws into the tree. Well the food is safe now and far enough from the camp that we shouldn't have visitors. So let us go and get our dishes washed."

"Ahhh! I thought I could get out of washing dishes out here."

"Not unless you want a wild animal coming to visit you while you are sleeping."

"I will wash," Peter said hurriedly.

"While you are at it, wash your face or animals will be waking you up when they lick your face to get the chocolate on it."

After the chores were done, they sat down by the camp fire again. Peter had got into his pajamas and had a blanket wrapped around him to keep warm.

"Dad, I don't see this many stars in the sky at home. Why?"

"In the city, you are surrounded by lights that hide the stars from view."

"I read that the explorer's used the stars to guide them."

"Lie down on your back and look to your right. Do you see the Big Dipper sometimes called Ursa Major?"

"You mean the arrangement of stars that look like a big pot?"

"Yes, see the two stars at the front of the pot."

"Yes."

"Now look straight up from those two stars and keep going till you see the Little Dipper or Ursa Minor. The last star in the handle of the Little Dipper is called Polaris or the North Star. It never moves. All the other stars rotate around it. It sits over the North Pole so explorers could always tell which way was north."

"How do you know all this?"

"In the Yukon, we have lots of time to look at the night sky," his father chuckled.

"I forgot able the long nights and long days up there."

"Right now it is spring, our days are getting longer and we only have a few hours of dark. In fact some days, you can actually see the moon at ten and eleven o'clock in the morning up in the beautiful sun lit sky. We even have midnight baseball games with no park lights."

Peter gave a big yawn, then said, "You do,"

"We do. I think it is about time for us to say good night. Six o'clock is going to come early for you."

They climbed into the tent zipping the door flap closed. Peter rolled his sleeping bag out beside his father's and climbed into it. His father gave him a kiss good night and before long Peter drifted into a sound sleep.

CHAPTER 5

The next morning, Peter woke to the shrill squawks of a multitude of birds. He stretched and quickly wiggled out of his sleeping bag when he realized his father was already up. He dressed and crawled out of the tent.

The sky was ablaze with a multitude of colors. Peter had never seen the sky looks so beautiful. He began to understand why his father loved being out in nature so much.

Peter went behind some bushes to relieve himself. He noticed that the birds were darting around making a lot of noise but they didn't seem to be landing on the trees. Peter thought that was strange and wondered what had upset them so much.

Fear struck him when the idea popped into his head that some wild animal was hiding in the bushes ready to attack him and that was what upset the birds. He ran to the water's edge away from the trees. This way he could see the animal coming for him and he could jump in the pond and swim away from the animal. He had forgotten his father had told him to climb a tree. He wondered where his father was. Had the wild animal already attached him? Peter felt panicky as he stood there waiting for the worst to happen.

Fear built in Peter with every minute that passed until he spotted his father coming into view. He was on the cliff above the waterfall. Relief filled Peter as his father waved at him and started climbing down the steep incline. Peter ran over to his father.

"Where did you go?" Peter asked trying to keep from showing his father how scared he had been.

"I took a walk around and found a lot of animal tracks going down the mountain. It is like a mass exodus but I don't understand why they are doing it. Usually it is because they smell a forest fire and are running for their lives. That is why I went to higher ground to see if I could see any signs of a fire and there is nothing. I also noticed that the water is higher. So I walked upstream. I thought of a flash flood but it hasn't rained so I ruled that out. Then I wondered if a beaver dam had given way somewhere upstream but I didn't see anything. The only thing I did see was that injured wolf. He is moving down the mountain also. He is very thin so I know he is hungry so he is dangerous. We will have to keep an eye out for him."

"Should we pack up and leave," Peter said feeling very uneasy about the wolf and the odd behaviour of the other animals.

"No, I don't see any danger. I think everything will be fine. I don't get to take my boy fishing to often so let's go and catch our breakfast," his father said as he messed Peter's hair up.

"How are we going to catch fish? You didn't bring any fishing rods," Peter asked as they walked back to the tent.

"Didn't I? Watch this." His father dragged his pack out of the tent. He unlaced a two foot tube that was tied to it. He opened the one end and dumped out two fishing rods that broke down into three two foot pieces each. His father quickly assembled them.

"What are we using for bait?"

"While a certain person was sawing logs, I was finding worms," his father said with a smile on his face as he picked up a small contain by the side of the tent.

Peter really didn't want to touch these dirty, slimy, squirmy, creatures but he knew he didn't have a choice if he wanted to impress his father. His father showed him how to put the worm on a hook so the fish couldn't steal it. Peter followed his example and went to the water's edge and threw his line in.

Peter sat down on a rock and pulled a book out of his coat pocket and began to read.

"What is that for?" his father said as he pointed at the book.

"I thought I would read while I wait for a fish to bite."

"If you have your face in a book all the time, you are going to miss things in the world around you."

"What do you mean?"

"Well like that eagle that just flew into sight."

The eagle let out a loud screech as it dove low dragging it's talons in the water. It then rose into the air with a large fish squirming on its claws.

"Boy, I wish we could fish like that. I am getting hungry," Peter exclaimed.

"Will this help," his father said as he pulled some pepperoni sticks from his vest pocket. "Catch."

Peter was soon munching away on the pepperoni sticks but he was finding it boring just sitting there. He wanted to get back to his book. He was in the most exciting part of it where the young boy is hiding in the rocks from the Indians who had attacked his family's homestead. Yet he didn't want to upset his father so he sat there wishing a fish would bite so they could eat.

Two black headed birds riding low in the water moving downstream caught Peter's attention.

"What kind of birds are they, Dad?"

"Those are loons, the bird that is on our dollar coins."

One of the birds dove underwater coming up several minutes later with a fish in its mouth. It quickly ate it and dove under again.

"Wow, did you see that," exclaimed Peter.

The other loon swam toward its companion and let out its haunting call.

"Dad, Look Dad, is that a baby loon on that loon's back?"

"Baby loons are a food source for many land animals. Loon's legs are so far back on their body they are awkward on land so their only defense is to stab their enemies with their sharp beaks. Land animals can move fast so they can take the baby loons before they get stabbed. So adult loons take their babies with them in the water where they are swift and can protect them."

The loons swam downriver disappearing from sight.

"That is strange," his father said as he scratched his head.

"What is?"

"Usually loons don't go far from their nests but those birds look like they are leaving the area also.

"Oh…oh," Peter exclaimed as he felt a fish pull on his line. "I think I have a bite."

"Pull slowly back on the line. Then start reeling the line in."

Peter did as he was told and the fish leaped out of the water fighting to get away. Peter struggled to pull the fish in. Ten minutes later, a beautiful big rock bass was lying on the ground beside him still attached to the hook.

"Dad, he is a big fish isn't he," Peter bubbled with excitement.

"He is a beauty. He will make a good meal but first a picture of your first fish. Stand in front of that big tree and hold the fish up," his father said as he pulled a small camera from one of his vest pockets.

Peter did what he was told and his father took several pictures of his first catch. Peter was thinking that he would be able to brag to his friends about his fish and when they doubted the size he would be able to pull out the picture and prove to them he had caught such a large fish.

"Now let's eat." His father unhooked the fish. He pulled his knife out of the sheath on his belt and began filleting the fish.

"Peter, go and get the fire started."

After six tries, Peter had the fire going. His father placed a flat rock beside the flames and waited till it got very hot. He then got the fish frying on the hot rock as well as water boiling for coffee and oatmeal.

Peter excitedly talked about his struggle to bring the fish to shore while his father sat back smiling and enjoying his son's excitement over his accomplishment. Eventually, he took off his vest and wiped the sweat off his forehead. "Are you hot?" he asked Peter.

"Yea, it does seem hotter than it did yesterday."

"It sure is," his father said wiping more sweat from his face before he dished out their food and they ate looking over the pond and listening to the splashing of the water over the rocks of the nearby waterfall. "I was thinking that you could learn to shoot a bow and arrow this morning.

"Yes," Peter said with excitement. "I can't wait to try."

"I will set up a target," his father said as he got up and went over to the tent and pulled out a paper target from his pack. He went to a nearby tree and hung it up. He went back to the tent and pulled out the bow and quiver of arrows. Peter was anxious to try it but he was also scared that he would fail and disappoint his father. He nervously walked over to the place his father said he would shot from. "Peter, you have to notch the arrow this way," his father said as he showed Peter how to place the arrow in the bow. "Then you pull straight back aiming at the target and release the arrow," his father said as he placed Peter's hands in the right place on the bow and showed him how to pull the bow string and arrow back. The string was so tight it took all of Peter's strength to pull it back and hold it. "Now release." Peter watched as the arrow went speeding through the air toward the target. It missed the target and landed in the ground somewhere behind the tree but his father praised him for the effort. Peter spent the next two hours sending arrow after arrow toward the target then spending time finding all the arrows so he could do it all over again. His father sat and watched commenting here and there on how Peter could do it better. Eventually, Peter was hitting the target. His father praised him and Peter felt on top of the world. His arms were aching with the strain but he didn't care he had done it.

They then went swimming because the temperature was rising. They splashed and played like river otters for over half an hour before his father said he was tired and headed for shore. As he climbed out of the water, he noticed several frogs heading away from the pond. He had never seen anything like that before. A large flock of birds of all kinds flew away overhead. What is going on he wondered? This was not natural behaviour for the animals. Should they head back to civilization, he wondered but he was having such a good time with his son he didn't want to spoil it.

Butch got out bags of nuts, dried fruit, and beef jerky for lunch. "Peter, come and eat. We have to talk about something. I am a bit concerned at the way the animals and birds are acting. They know something that we as humans can't detect. I think we have to think about getting out of here. I really don't want to because I am having a great time with you but I have to think of your safety first."

"I hate to leave because I am having a great time but it is strange that all the animals are leaving. Did you see those snakes slithering into the woods?"

"No, when did you see that?"

"When I got out of the water, I went behind some trees and went to the washroom. I saw about six of them. Also have you noticed that the birds had quieted down?"

"A large flock of birds left the area while you were still in the water. If we pack up now, we can get back to the ranger's station just after dark. I will get the tent packed up. Can you get the canteens filled with water for the walk out of here?"

"Sure, Dad," Peter said feeling a little sad about leaving. He went and got the canteens and walked slowly to the pond. When he got down to the water he noticed that the rock he had sat on while fishing was now underwater. Peter realized that the sound of the waterfalls was louder. When he saw a spout of water like a mini fountain spraying up in the air, Peter felt very scared. What was happening? He quickly filled the canteens and began hurrying back toward his father who was packing up the gear.

Peter didn't get far when the ground began to move under his feet. The tremor built until Peter was thrown off balance and fell. He landed on the ground with a thud. The canteens fell out of his hands and did a silly dance as the earth's vibration moved them across the ground.

The tremor was so strong that the trees began to sway and bang into each other. The sound of wood slamming into wood filled the air. Then the cracking of breaking branches began. Branches and leaves started falling around them. Peter saw his father fall just as a very loud cracking and snapping sound occurred. A large tree teetered for a few seconds before it crashed to the ground. More trees began to fall as the tangled roots were pulled from the rocky ground as the earth moved more and more violently.

Peter rolled out of the way as a large branch crashed down within inches of his head. The small branches whipped his face and arms stinging him. He huddled near a large rock for shelter. He was too frightened to move. Tears soaked his face as he prayed that his father was all right. He realized it was an earthquake which he had learned about in school but he never realized the damage it could do until now. It seemed to go on forever then suddenly it stopped. The earth stopped moving and the trees slowly stopped swaying. The noise slowly died until all Peter heard was the sound of water gurgling and splashing over the waterfall. He expected to hear his father call him but no call came.

Peter slowly uncurled and wiggled out from under the debris that had fallen around him. Shock set in when he saw the devastation that surrounded him. Tree branches, trees, and leaves covered the ground. Large tree roots stuck up here and there. Other trees leaned against their neighboring trees for support.

Peter called his father's name several times with no response. He began struggling over branches and tree trunks as he headed toward where he last saw his father. He found him lying very still with a tree trunk pinning his leg. He also had a broken branch lying across his chest and a bump on his head.

CHAPTER 6

He was so pale and lay so still, Peter thought his father was dead. He tentatively reached out to find the pulse in his father's neck scared that his father would be cold and lifeless. When he felt the thump, thump, thump under his fingers a huge feeling of relief swept over him. Tears rolled down his face and as he sank down beside his father and tried to shake him to wake him. Nothing happened.

He sat back on his heels as he tried to think of what he should do. His mind didn't seem to want to work. There was no one around to help him. Peter never felt so lonely and scared in all his life. Then his stepfather's words popped into his head, *you are a reader so you can draw on the knowledge you have learned from books.*

What do people do in books when someone is hurt? Peter thought. They keep the person warm. Peter jumped up and scrambled over to the collapsed tent. He wiggled into it and grabbed a sleeping bag. He pulled as hard as he could. It seemed to be caught on something. He gave it another hard tug. He heard a ripping sound and it came free. He squirmed back out of the tent dragging the sleeping bag behind him and rushed back to his father's side. He tried to cover him but the tree branch on his chest was in the way. Peter didn't know what to do. Would he hurt his father if he moved the tree branch?

Peter saw the large bump on his father's head. The area was beginning to swell. What stops swelling? Then he remembered the school nurse had used ice when he was hit by the school bully. He didn't have ice but the pond water was cool. He stripped off his shirt and made his way to the pond carefully climbing over tree trunks and broken branches. He dunked the shirt in to the water and scurried back to his father leaving a trail of water behind him. He put the wet shirt on his father's head. The shock of the cool water running down his face brought his father around.

"Are you all right, Dad?"

"Can't breathe…chest hurts," his father gasped.

"I will get the branch off you," Peter said as he started throwing the debris off of him. He grabbed the large branch and used every bit of his strength to lift it off his father's chest. Now he had to get the tree trunk off his father's leg but first he covered his father with the sleeping bag.

"Is that better, Dad?"

"Easier…to breathe…but still hurts," gasped his father.

"We have to get your leg out," Peter said as he tried to figure out a way to do it.

"Get branch…try to…pry it up."

Peter got a stout branch and tried to do what his father said but he couldn't move it.

Peter spotted his father's hatchet lying on the ground nearby. "Dad, I will cut the trunk into a smaller piece then we can move it."

He took the hatchet and swung it with all his might. He barely made a cut in the tree. His father let out a painful yell and grabbed his leg. There had to be another way.

Then Peter remembered the mining story he had read a few months before. The miners had been in a cave in and they dug their buddy out from under one of the support beams that had fallen on him. They dug around him and pulled him free.

Peter immediately began to dig around his father's leg but the ground was hard and rocky. His fingers were soon torn and bleeding trying to get through this packed rocky earth.

"Dad, lie still. I am going to find something to dig with."

His father nodded, lay back, and closed his eyes.

Peter began a frantic search of the campsite. He finally found a metal spoon. He hurried back to his father and began frantically digging. It seemed like hours to him before he was able to move a rock that had pinned his father's leg up against the tree trunk.

"Dad, try to move yourself backward while I pull you."

"Will…try," his father gasped as he sat up and tried to brace his arms to push himself backward. Peter grabbed his father under the arms and pulled while his father moaned as he weakly tried to move himself. His leg came free showing them a large bloody gash over the area where the leg lay at an odd angle.

Butch's survival instincts took over. "Peter…get…first aid kit…sewing kit…my pack," his father struggled to say.

Peter found his father's pack and returned to his father's side with these items.

"Need to…straighten leg…clean…sew gash"

"Me," squeaked Peter looking panicky.

"Blood…attracts…animals," his father panted, "Hungry wolf."

"Oh…ok," Peter said feeling sick to his stomach. He had to help his father and he definitely didn't want animals attacking them but could he do the things his father was asking him to do. He realised that he had to if they were going to survive.

Peter realized that his father's leg was broken. He remembered reading that you had to pull the leg straight and then brace it from moving out of position. He found a pair of his father's jeans and ripped it in strips. He also found three fairly straight branches and ripped the leaves and small branches off of them. He came back to his father's side and knelt down.

 "Ok," Peter said feeling scared to death. "Are you ready, Dad?"

His father grabbed a twig and put it in his mouth and bit down. He nodded his head yes.

Peter was shaking as he took hold of his father's lower leg and pulled and slowly turned it. Peter suddenly felt the bones snap into place. His father let out a scream of pain. Peter tied three sticks to his father's leg using the strips of material.

"Stop…bleeding," his father mumbled.

Peter washed the gash out like his mother did when he hurt himself. He realized that his father needed stitches. He had never sewn before but he remembered watching his grandmother do something that she called cross stitch. He felt thousands of butterflies in his stomach as he threaded the needle with the white cotton thread that was in the sewing kit. He tied a knot in the end of it like his grandmother had and gritted his teeth as he shoved the needle into his father's flesh. With irregular stitches he closed the gash in his father's leg with a line of x's like his grandmother had done. He then smeared the antibiotic cream he had found in the first aid kit on the gash and bandaged the area. All the while his father grimaced in pain with every stitch.

"Peter…cut bloody…pants away…bury it deep…smell of blood…brings animals."

Peter did what his father said. He went a good distance from the camp and buried all the pieces of material with blood on it. He then covered the area with rocks. He hoped that was deep enough to keep animals away. He then returned to his father's side unsure of what to do next.

His father was is pain so Peter gave his father two aspirins and a drink of water and told him to rest as he looked around trying to salvage what he could of the camp site.

He figured that the rangers wouldn't come until they were late returning. That would be about six days. His father needed medical attention now. What could he do? They would need shelter, food, and protection until help came. He decided that shelter was the most important if he was to keep his father warm. He inspected the tent but there was no way to get it free from the tree trunk that lay on one corner of the tent.

Instead he took his father's knife and cut as much as he could away from the trunk. He then found two y-shaped branches that he pounded into the ground at each end of his father. He then laid a straight branch into the whys and tied it in tightly with fishing line. He then draped the tent material across the branch and used rocks to hold the sides down. It was crude but it would keep them dry.

They would need food. He went looking for the food bag hanging in the tree but he couldn't find it. He began searching the ground around where it had been hanging. He found the bag in tatters. There were only a few plastic bags of dried vegetables and meat that were not torn open. This wouldn't last long, Peter thought as he went back to his father's side carrying the meager food supplies with him.

He remembered a story about an East Coast fisherman who used a weir to catch fish. It was worth a try he thought. He chopped a bunch of branches and sharpened the ends. He waded into the cold water where the river current was a bit stronger and pounded the sticks in a sac shape with a rock. Hopefully a fish would swim in but it could not turn around and swim back out. He also set up two long poles into the ground and tied long lengths of fishing lines with hooks with bait and sinkers at the end. He also found the bow and a few arrows that had not been smashed. Could he hunt a small animal for food?

He cleared the area around his make shift tent and moved the fire pit closer to it. He got a fire going and made a pot of stew like his father had done the night before. He remembered reading that animals didn't like fire so he wanted to keep a good sized fire going. Peter knew he only had a few hours of light left so he started piling up wood for the camp fire. As he worked he kept thinking of the wolf that may still be in the area. Would the wolf try to attack them? How could he protect his father? He knew fire scared wild animals but if he was out hunting and the fire went out, who would protect his father.

Then an idea blossomed into his head. If he drove posts into the ground and weaved the branches in and out like a basket weave. He could build a kind of fence around the camp. It would give them some kind of protection. He immediately started building his fence with all the downed branches and tree trunks in the area. He then remembered that Africans natives sometimes used pointed sticks coming out of the ground in the bottom of pits. They cover the pit up and wait for the animal to fall in on the sticks impaling them. He wouldn't dig a pit but if the animal jumped over his fence they could land on the sticks. He thought he would give it a try. He began sharpening sticks and pounded them into the ground with the points sticking up in the air ready to impale any intruder.

He was exhausted and starving by the time he was done but at least he felt a bit safer. He checked on his father who was sleeping. Peter touched his father gently on the head. His father was a little hot but he seemed to be resting peacefully even though his breathing still seemed laboured. Peter remembered reading that willow bark was good for fevers but he couldn't remember what you did with it. He sat down by the fire and ate some stew. He was exhausted and scared as the darkness began to spread around him. He got comfortable in front of the tent with the hatchet, knife and bow and arrows sitting beside him. He soon dosed off into a fitful sleep as the moon came up.

Peter snapped awake when he heard a wolf howl nearby. He grabbed a few pieces of wood and built the fire up. He then took a longer stick and lit the end to use as a torch. He got up carrying the burning stick in one hand and the hatchet in the other and walked around the walled in area staring out into the darkness.

Was the wolf close by? Was it looking for an easy meal? Had he smelled his father's blood? Then he saw two bright eyes looking at him from a nearby bush. Was it the wolf or another hungry predator? He then remembered that he had not washed his dishes or emptied the pot of leftover stew. Peter swung the burning stick and yelled hoping it would scare the animal away. It did but for how long?

He hurried to the fire and dumped the remaining stew into the fire. He then took the dirty dishes and scrubbed them with dirt hoping that it would kill the smell of food. The bags of food he put in the first aid tin and buried it next to the campfire. He hoped that would keep the animals away.

Chapter 7

Peter sat by the tent struggling to keep awake. He was afraid the wolf would attack when he was asleep. He struggled to think of things he could do to get them out of there. How could they stay here six days or more if that wild animal was after them? He didn't think the wall he made would keep the animal out for long but it was the best he could do. What should he do? The need for sleep muddled his thinking. His thoughts seemed to go round and round in circles.

His father called out in a faint voice, "Peter, can…I have…water."

Peter crawled into the tent beside his father with the canteen he had filled earlier. He lifted his father's head and put the canteen to his father's lips. His father was burning up with fever. Peter found the bottle of aspirins he had tossed into his father's back pack. They had six of them left. That would not last until help came. He took out two and had his father take them with water.

Peter then settled down in front of the tent again with his arsenal around him. He had to stay awake and protect his father. He also had to figure out what to do next.

He thought about what his father had said about the North Star. He lay on his back and stared at the stars trying to find it. When he did, he realized that if he followed it, it would lead them deeper into the wilderness.

How could he do it anyway? He could only see the stars at night and night time was not the time to wander around in the woods with wild animals. His father was not able to get up and walk. He couldn't carry his father. He wondered about a travois like the Indians used but with all the trees down and the ones leaning on each other. It would be dangerous and difficult. Would he have enough strength to drag his father on a travois?

He couldn't leave his father to get help because a wild animal might attack him. He didn't know the way back anyway. He had already tried to use his father's phone but there was no reception where they were. Peter got up again and walked around the perimeter of his small enclosed area. He didn't see anything this time but he felt like something out there was watching him.

How could he move his father? Then he thought of a raft like in "Huckleberry Finn." He had just finished reading this story two weeks before. He wondered if he could make a raft like the picture in the book. He had fishing line and the rope his father had used for the food bag to tie the raft together. Peter sat thinking about this idea. It was the only way he could think of to move his father. He had a lot of wood laying around them he could cut into poles to make the raft. He only needed a few longer ones. He decided that at first light he would get started on building a raft. He just hoped it would float. He remembered reading that people always settled near a source of water. He just hoped that was true and he would find help quickly somewhere along the river.

As the night grew colder, Peter sat shivering and struggling to stay awake. He could not remember ever staying up this late before. He recited nursery rhymes, he tried to remember jokes he had heard at school. He even recited the times tables and tried to remember history dates as a means to keep his mind awake. Several times he dozed off and awoke abruptly when he heard a twig snap or the fire spark which he kept burning brightly.

He finally fell into a deep sleep around dawn but his sleep was disturbed when the earth began to shake again as a small tremor passed through it. This terrified him when a few of the leaning trees fell to the ground with loud thuds that rang through the woods. This terrified him. He realized that it would not be safe to go through the woods if another tremor occurred. He had to get them out of there by water. He had no other choice.

Peter had hoped that his father could advise him on the best way to construct the raft but when he checked on him his father was delirious. His fever was high and he called Peter, Sam who had been his father's best friend as a boy. This just added to Peter's anxiety. He had to get his father out of there.

He began laying out several seven foot poles on the ground beside each other. He tied them tightly together. He tied a four foot pole across them about every two feet apart. He remembered his teacher saying that a triangle was the strongest structure so he tied other poles on a slant between the four foot poles. He then added two seven foot poles on each side to form the sides of the triangles. He struggled to pry the one side of the raft up so he could flip it so the flat side was up. When he accomplished this he sat down exhausted. He ate some beef jerky and then faced his next challenge of getting his father and the raft to the water's edge.

Peter had read about the early East Coast Canadian fishermen who used logs to roll their boats in and out of the water. He found three logs about the same width and put them under the raft. He then took the tent material down and laid it on the raft.

Now he had to get his father onto it. He tried to lift his father under the arms and drag him but his father moaned in pain. So he stopped because he didn't want to hurt him more than he already was. He then rolled him onto the raft and got him centered on it. Peter than wrapped the sleeping bag around his father and brought the tent material over it to keep him as dry and warm as possible. He tied his father onto the raft so he would not fall off.

He took a deep breath and thought here goes. He cleared a path to the water's edge and started rolling the raft slowly toward the water's edge. As the logs beneath the raft rolled out at the top, Peter would grab it and take it to the foot of the raft and roll the raft back onto it. Peter repeatedly moved the logs as one after the other rolled out the top of the raft and put it at the bottom of the raft as he moved it slowly to the water's edge.

This was it. Would the raft float? He pushed it into the water and the raft lifted off the rollers. Peter let out a yell of victory as he waded into the water after it.

He tried sitting down on the edge of the raft but it sank low into the water. He decided he would have to walk behind it since the current kept trying to turn it sideways. Peter tied the raft to a rock as it floated at the water's edge. He realized that he may be in the water a long time and he would have to keep warm. Peter remembered reading about how a diver's wet suit works. It lets a thin layer of water into the suit and traps it there. The water is heated by the diver's body heat and insulates him from the cold. Could he improvise and make a wet suit out of things he had? He took his yellow rain slicker out of his backpack. It was rubbery like a wet suit and could protect his main body but what about his legs. He thought about it for a while and then it occurred to him that if he took pieces of the ground sheet and tied them around his legs it might work.

He put a layer of warm clothes on which should hold the water against his body. He then put on his rain coat and tied the cuffs tight around his wrists to keep himself warm. He then folded the coats excess material between his legs. He found a roll of electrical tape in his father's backpack and taped the material into place. Peter took rope and tied it around his waist and pulled the tail of the rope between his legs and tied it to the rope around his waist like a harness. He then took pieces of ground sheet and tied them around his legs. He took his shoes off and put plastic bags on his feet and ties them on. He then puts his shoes back on. He grabbed his backpack that he had filled with item he thought they may need on this journey and put it on his back. He waded into the water and felt the water seep in next to his skin.

Peter tied himself to the raft and began guiding the raft into the downstream current. He stopped at the weir and the fishing poles to see if he had caught anything. He found a seven-inch fish in the weir. He caught it and killed it with his father's knife which he put back in the sheath on his belt. He put the fish into a plastic bag and shoved it into his backpack. He took one last look at their campsite before he started the long trek downstream. He hoped he was doing the right thing.

Chapter 8

Peter noticed that his strange garb was helping to keep warm water trapped against his body. Unfortunately, he had nothing to help his hands which started to feel cold once he got into the fast moving river current. He was glad he had tied himself to the raft because he was able to stop every so often. So he could blow hot air on his hands or put them under his arm pits to warm them.

The current gently helped push him and the raft downstream. Peter walked slowly and carefully because the rocks below his feet were moss covered and very slippery. He had to watch that he didn't stumble over large rocks or submerged logs. Some of the rocks shifted when he stepped on them so travelling was slow.

As he waded onward down the river, the sun came up over the trees and beamed down on him. Sweat started pouring off of him in his make shift rubber suit on top yet the lower part of him felt cool all at the same time. It felt so strange.

The sun light danced on the water making him squint. He wished now he had his cap and sunglasses his mother had insisted he bring. He hadn't seen or even thought about them since the earthquake. He could feel the skin on his face begin to burn.

He moved along slowly hoping around every bend to see any sign of another human being. His father lay in front of him with sweat beads on his forehead. Peter had given his father the remaining aspirins before they left but it wasn't helping much.

Occasionally, he would stop and put his wet cold hands to his father's forehead to cool his father down but his father became hot and hotter. Then Peter realized that he had wrapped his father in a sleeping bag and the tent material, he was dressed to warm with the sun beating down on him. Peter stopped in shallow water and untied his father's wrappings. He removed the sleeping bag and rewrapped his father in the tent material. He rolled the sleeping bag up and stuffed it under the tent between his father's legs. After that he noticed that his father was more comfortable because he fell into a deep sleep.

Minutes turned into hours as he trudged along. The only thing that encouraged him was when he started seeing little animals and birds. First there were two robins sitting on a tree branch that extended over the water. A little while later, an eagle soared high over his head screeching with joy as he rode the air currents. Then he spotted two turtles sunbathing on a large rock that jutted out into the river. Even a few fish swam past him and darted away with a flick of their tails. He saw two loons with their baby swimming upstream. He wondered if there were the same loons he had saw with his father. The sight of all these creatures encouraged him because that meant the tremors were over.

The toll of the cold water started to affect him. He had walked miles with the cold water pushing him along in its rush to the sea. His whole body ached with fatigue and he was exhausted from lack of sleep. His hands and feet were starting to turn cold and numb. He didn't know how much farther he could walk. His stomach was growling and he knew he had to stop soon before he collapsed but where?

Peter was afraid to stop because he had caught glimpses of a dark greyish creature moving in and out of the trees along the shoreline. Was the wolf following him? If it was the wolf, he couldn't outrun it.

CHAPTER 9

Two hours later, Peter was struggling as the current was getting stronger which wanted to push the raft faster than Peter was able to go. He fought to keep on his feet as the current kept trying to lift him up and sweep him and the raft downstream. This was tiring him out even more. He didn't know how much farther he could go but he had to. His father was burning up with fever. He wanted to rest but he was scared to go ashore because ten minutes before he had seen a thin wolf standing on a rock looking at him. Was it the same wolf he wondered?

As the raft turned a bend in the river, Peter saw a tree which had fallen into the river. Its roots stuck out of the ground inches from the water's edge and fanned out six feet wide. Its trunk stretched out another ten feet out into the river before it submerged completely other than branches sticking out here and there. The river's current swirled around the branches rustling the few leaves that were remaining on the waterlogged branches. When Peter got to it, he noticed that the trunk had caused a small calm area where the current couldn't reach.

Peter decided that this was a good place to stop. He didn't think that the wolf would walk out on the tree trunk. He carefully pushed the raft over the submerged part of the tree and climbed over it. Peter pushed the raft into the calm water and untied himself from the raft. He tied it to the tree. He took his backpack off and laid it on the tree trunk. This gave him the freedom to climb on the tree trunk and laid his back against a branch that was sticking up in the air. The leaves of the branch rustled over his head offering him some shade from the sun's beams. He was so tired that all he wanted was to sleep.

He reached for his backpack and pulled it toward himself. He found the fish in it that he had gotten out of the weir. He couldn't cook it here but he had remembered that when his family went to a Chinese restaurant, his step-father had showed him sushi. He had explained to Peter that it was raw fish wrapped in seaweed and that a lot of people ate it. Peter couldn't think of anything so disgusting at the time but right now he was so hungry, raw fish sounded delicious to him. He took his father's knife and tried to fillet the fish like his father had done the day before. He then picked up a piece of the meat. He smelt it, then put it in his mouth and began to chew. It wasn't anything he would want to eat all the time but it was food and he was starving.

He was just putting another piece of meat in his mouth when he heard a twig snap. He looked up to see two yellowish eyes watching him from the tree line. The wolf cautiously moved toward the downed tree.

Peter was terrified. How was he going to get away from this animal? Should he try to shoot it with the bow and arrow that was tied to his backpack? If he just injured the wolf, he knew it would get more aggressive. The wolf walked behind the tree root out of Peter's sight. Peter watched the wolf step into the water and jump up onto the tree trunk and slowly approached him. Peter had to get his father out of there. He slid off the tree grabbing his backpack which he threw onto the raft. He untied it quickly moved it away from the tree and into the current. Peter tied himself to the raft again and moved into deeper water. Would the wolf come in the water after them?

Peter kept glancing over his shoulder watching the wolf as he pushed the raft quickly downstream. It had made its way out on the tree trunk and was gobbling up the fish remains that Peter had not gotten a chance to eat.

It then looked out at where Peter and his father were and let out a growl before he returned to the shoreline and began following them along the river bank.

Peter was scared so he moved farther out into the river. The current was stronger there and he had to fight to keep his footing. The current pushed and whirled around them wanting to take him and the raft swiftly downstream. Peter kept watching the shore where the wolf was keeping up to them. Peter panicked when he realized that he had only a few more hours before darkness would set in. He couldn't stay in the water all night but the wolf was waiting on the shore for him and his father. He was to tired and weak from hunger. The only solution he could come up with was to cross to the opposite shore.

Peter began steering the raft diagonally across the river. He had only taken about fifteen steps when the ground under his feet dropped away. Peter leaned on the raft beside his father's head and tried to steer the raft as he kicked his feet. However, the river had a different idea. The river began pushing the raft faster and faster downstream keeping the raft away from the shores. The more Peter struggled to get to the opposite shore the more the river's current pushed him into the center of the river.

Fifteen minutes later, the river began to narrow into a long rock canyon with steep walls. The water became more and more choppy and swifter moving. The raft spun and bounced along with Peter clinging to it with all his might. Water splashed over them as they sped down the river leaving the wolf behind.

The river began having large rocks jutting out from the swift water which swirled around them. Unfortunately, the raft wasn't as agile and it hit one rock so hard it almost flipped over. Peter was torn from the raft and his should smashes into a rock as the raft spun in its race downstream.

The rope that tied Peter to the raft pulled at his waist as the raft dragged him spinning and twisting as it careened onward. He struggled to get his head out of the water so he could get air. His lungs burned as the need for air grew in him. Peter swallowed water as he was dragged under time and time again. Peter tried several times to he tried to grab the raft and get his upper body onto it but he did not succeed. The raft smashed into another rock and Peter hoped it would not break apart. He would not be able to save his father if it happened. He didn't even know if he would survive this as he went under again swallowing more water.

The river careened around a sharp bend to the right in the canyon wall. The raft and Peter was thrown leftward onto a rocky ledge that jutted out a few feet underwater. Peter coughing and choking scrambled to his knees and grabbed the raft pushing it out of the current onto the small beach that existed just in front of the forty foot canyon walls that surrounded them.

Peter felt his father's head and realized his fever was down because of the cold water that had soaked them both. "Dad, are you all right?"

"Co…cold," his father opened his eyes and said between chattering teeth.

"Me too, we lost the matches. They were in my backpack and it is gone. I could try to start a fire with sticks rubbed together like the Indians used to. It will take a while," Peter said as he started untying the ground sheets from his father's legs to get the sleeping bag to cover his father.

"Inside…vest…pocket," His father said as he struggled for air, "Hard… time…breathing." His father started trying to get to his vest but he was tangled in the tent material and the ropes that tied him to the raft.

"You have matches on you," Peter said as he sat there shivering.

"Always…be…prepared," his father gasped.

Peter got the small watertight container of matches out of his father's pocket and covered his with the damp sleeping bag. He then began to gather pieces of wood and dried vegetation that had been thrown up on this small stretch of land by the rushing flood waters in spring. He then put rocks around the fire pit he built next to the canyon wall. He also looked for any way that the wolf could get down to where they were. He didn't see any way down the forty foot cliff that surrounded them. He then returned to his father's side.

"We don't have a lot of wood but if we can get the rocks heated we can use them like old fashion bed warmers," Peter said as he got the fire going. He soon took warm rocks and placed them under the sleeping bag to warm his father up.

"That should warm you up a bit until we can get out of here," Peter said as he looked down river. The canyon turned again about five hundred feet away. Peter sat on his haunches wondering what to do. The only way out was to go back into the raging water but he was cold and tired and didn't have the strength to go on. Darkness was going to set in soon and the wolf was still out there. This was a good safe place to spend the night.

"Hun…gry," his father gasped.

"Me too, but we haven't anything to eat," Peter said as he added another piece of wood to the fire.

"Other…poc..ket," His father gasped.

"What else have you got in there?"

"Energy…bars…for…emerg…ency," his father said as he weakly handed Peter a bar.

"You do believe in being prepared," Peter said as he smiled down at his father. He tore open the bar's packaging and took a bite. "These are not so bad," Peter said after he swallowed his mouthful. He opened his father's bar for him and they ate in silence.

"Dad, we are safe here from the wolf but we are still in danger. I don't know if coming down the river was such a good idea. I never even considered that the river would be anything but a gentle stream all the way down the mountain. Now we have to get back in this swirling water tomorrow just to get out of this canyon and there could be a waterfall around the next bend. I am scared."

"Did good....only way...out."

"We still may encounter that wolf. I don't know if I can protect you." Peter continued telling his father about his fears. He didn't notice that his father had drifted off. When Peter realized it, it was dark and cold out. He climbed under the sleeping bag beside his father and cuddled up for warmth. He was soon in a dead sleep caused by exhaustion.

Chapter 10

Peter woke to the sound of birds singing and the water gurgling and splashing as it raced downriver. He tried to crawl out of the sleeping bag without disturbing his father who seemed to be in a deep sleep. He had to get his father help today.

Peter was scared to go back into the water but he knew he had to. It was the only way out of this canyon. He again tied the pieces of ground sheet to his legs and rearranged the rope that tied his raincoat around his torso. There were small rips in the ground sheet pieces but it could offer him some protection in the water. He then tied himself to the raft again. He pushed it back out off the little ledge.

This time he lay on the raft between his father's legs with his legs dragging in the water. The raft rode low in the water. He just hoped that they could make it out of there. Would the raft hold together if they hit more rough water? He had to try. He almost drowned yesterday when he was being dragged behind the raft and didn't want that to happen again.

It took seconds for the current to grab the raft and start it careening down the river. Peter tried to steer using his legs like a rudder as they sped toward the next bend in the river. Again the raft was thrown toward the canyon wall as the river bent in a tight arc.

Peter frantically tried to steer the raft away from the wall but the one corner of the raft hit jarring them and almost throwing Peter in the water. He heard a cracking sound as one of the logs in the raft broke in two. The raft began to list to that side as the raft spun and continued careening down the river backwards. He held on with all his might as they continued bouncing and spinning down the river with no control.

Peter was thrown into a rock which caught him on the arm cutting a deep gash. His father was laying on a slant when one part of the split log worked its way out of its bindings and sped away on the current. The other piece twisted and dragged behind the raft hitting Peter's legs occasionally. Peter was scarred that the raft would break apart and he knew he wouldn't be able to save his father from drowning, If that happened he didn't even know if he could save himself. All he could do was hold on for dear life.

The raft continued on what seemed like hours bouncing and spinning out of control until finally it was spewed out into a slower moving current as the river widens as it drops into a valley with trees growing right to the shoreline.

Exhausted Peter clung to the raft trying to figure out what to do. They were still drifting slowly downstream. His arm was hurting but the bleeding had finally stopped. His father lay shivering and moaning.

He had seen some deer drinking water at the shore line peacefully. Then the bushes moved near them and the deer ran into the trees. Was the wolf out there keeping up to their movement downstream? They were cold and wet. Peter would love to go to shore and build a fire to warm up but he was scared to. He knew he had no hope of fighting off the wolf with his hurt arm. All he could do was hold on and hope that he would find help soon.

Minutes turned to hours as the sun rose in the sky and warmed them. As they went Peter saw fish swim close to the raft. He wished he had a way to catch one. Peter's legs were numb with the cold of the water. He worried about his father who was not very responsive and his breathing seemed to be more laboured. Thirst set in as the sun beat down on them. When he tried to scoop some water up with his hand to get a drink, the raft tipped.

Peter quickly moved to straighten the raft and was afraid to move again.

Peter laid thinking of the little children's rhyme swirled around his head; *water, water everywhere and not a drop to drink.* The reflection of the sun on the surface of the water made him squint as he scoured the shoreline for any sign of humans. His mind went into a stupor as the hours ticked by. He didn't even notice the two rangers walking down the shoreline toward them when the raft came around a bend in the river.

The rangers spotted him and the tall one called out, "Hey kid, are you all right? Where did you come from?"

The sound of the voice, shocked Peter out of his stupor and he called out, "Help, help me." Peter tried to steer the raft as he kicked his feet to move the raft toward them. "My father is hurt. He needs a hospital."

The two rangers waded into the water to help him get the raft to shore. They helped him pull it up on the beach.

My name is Ben and my partner's name is Dan. What is your name?" asked the shorter ranger as he knelt down to examine Peter's father.

"Peter Davidson. That is my father, Butch Davidson," Peter said between chattering teeth.

"Where did your father and you come from?" asked the taller forest ranger.

"We were at my father's favorite fishing hole upstream near a small waterfall," Peter said as the ranger opened an emergency blanket up and wrapped it around Peter's shoulders.

"You came all that way on this raft."

"Yes, only way to get my father out of there he can't walk."

"How did you get around the white water in the canyon?"

"We didn't. We went right through it. That is where I got hurt."

"You were lucky. The last person who tried to go through that part of the river lost his life."

"We didn't have a choice. It was the only way I could move my father and I had to get him medical help. Also there is a wolf following us. I have seen it several times. It has a bad foot."

"That is not normal behaviour for a wolf. You say it is injured."

"I don't know what is normal but it has followed us for the last few days."

"What happened to your father?"

"A tree fell on his leg during the earthquake. His leg was broken. I tried to set it but he needs a doctor. Also one branch hit him across the chest and he is having trouble breathing?"

"What happened to your arm?"

"I hit a rock ledge as we went down the white rapids. I can't lift it up."

"Let me put it in a sling until we get you to the hospital and get it looked after," Dan said as he went down on one knee and looked through his backpack. He pulled out a long piece of material and expertly made a sling for Peter.

Ben had finished looking at Peter's father and took his radio out of his vest pocket. He called the ranger station and arranged for a helicopter to come and get them at a nearby clearing.

"We were out here looking for a poacher. You didn't see anyone did you," Ben asked.

"No, I did see a few deer at the river drinking and then they suddenly ran off into the woods. I thought the wolf had scared them."

"Peter, we have to walk about a mile to a clearing to be picked up. Do you think you can do that?"

"Yes, but do you have anything to eat and drink. I am starved."

"We should have thought of that," Ben said with a smile on his face. He pulled out some beef jerky and handed to Peter. He then unstrapped his canteen and opened it for Peter.

Peter gulped down some water and then tore into the beef jerky. It wasn't long before it was all gone. While he ate, the men took two of the raft poles and tied the tent material to them. They then moved Peter's father to this light weight stretcher. They gave him water and some aspirins that they had in their emergency kit.   He was covered in an emergency blanket tucked in around him. Peter took off his makeshift wet suit and pulled the aluminum emergency blanket around him tight to keep himself warm. They were ready for the walk to the landing place.

As they went Peter kept looking over his shoulder. He felt that the wolf was nearby watching them. At least now he was with two healthy adults who could protect them. He hurried to keep up with them. He didn't want to be left behind.

They climbed upward into the woods following a narrow trail before they came into a large clearing. It was covered in wild yellow flowers that smelt so fragrant. A helicopter came into view and settled down in the middle of the clearing. The smell of fuel and oil surrounded it as the blades started to slow down. The pilot climbed out when he saw them. They carefully loaded Peter's father into the helicopter and strapped him in. They put Peter near a window and showed him how to strap himself in. Dan handed him a pair of earphones to put on. When they were all in, and settled the pilot started the engine. Peter was not expecting it to be so noisy. He had never been up in a helicopter before and he was excited about it. He began to realize what a story he would have to tell his friends. He sat thinking about the journey he had just been through. His friends would never believe him.

As they rose into the sky, Peter saw the wolf standing there watching. It lowered its head like it was conceding to Peter that he had won. He had got them out of a very bad situation. A smile spread over his face. He had gotten his father to safety.

Chapter 11

When the helicopter landed on the roof of the tall brick hospital, they were met by doctors and nurses. His father was put onto a gurney and they hurried him through the sliding doors and into the elevator across the hall. Peter was led off in another direction to the children's ward where a team of doctors and nurses awaited him.

He had never had such a complete medical exam as he had that day. They checked him all over before they did minor surgery on his arm. He had cut the muscle in his arm and it needed to be reattached. He also had to warm up because his body temperature from all the cold water had dropped below normal. They had wrapped him in warmed blankets and heating pads around his legs that had been in the water so long.

Several hours later, his bed was rolled into a hospital room beside his father's bed. Peter had been told that his father's leg had been reset properly and he had had surgery because one of the broken ribs had punctured his lung. There were bags of medication handing on a hook over his father's head and a tube running down to his arm pumping antibiotics into his arm's vein.

"How are you doing, Peter?" his father said weakly. "You are going to have some story to tell your friends."

"They will never believe me," Peter said as he weakly smiled at his father. He was still feeling the effects of anesthetic. "I am just glad we made it."

"We wouldn't have if you hadn't kept your head and did everything you could to protect us. You are a true outdoorsman," his father said with a smile on his face. "I am so proud of you." Peter swelled with pride when he heard his father's words. He had proved to his father that he was more than a couch potato.

"As for your friends, when we get out of here we will take them to Canada Wonderland. You can tell them the story there and we can both show them our scars. They will have to believe you then."

"No water rides. I have had enough water for a while," Peter said as he rolled his eyes.

"Me too," his father laughed.

"What worries me more is what Mom is going to say? We will be lucky if she ever lets me go fishing with you ever again let alone going to Canada Wonderland," Peter said nervously.

"I expect that I will be in deep trouble," Butch said with a grimace.

"You sure are," Peter's mother said as she entered the room in a flurry with George following right behind her. "Peter, are you all right. You were supposed to keep him safe," she said as she turned toward Butch and started wagging her finger at him and telling him off. "See what you get when you want to sleep outside with wild animals…" She finally stopped when Butch cut in when she stopped to take a breath.

"How was I to know there was going to be an earthquake? That could have happened anywhere. Do you think I wished a tree to fall on me so I would endanger my son?" Butch tried to defend himself for his ex-wife's attack.

"Marianne, Marianne, calm down. You know Butch had no control of what happened," George said in a soothing voice trying to get his wife to calm down. "Just be glad they got to safety."

"Without Peter we wouldn't have got help. We would have most likely been a wolf's meal. He was amazing," his father said. "He came up with idea after idea that kept us safe."

"I just did what George told me to do."

"Me, what did I tell you. I know nothing about camping or fishing," George said.

"You told me that I was a reader and could draw from the knowledge I learned from books. That is how I came up with the idea of a raft to move Dad to safety otherwise we would still be in the woods fighting off that wolf."

"I guess George I have to thank you for getting my boy interested in reading books because without it we would be a wolf's dinner right now the way that creature followed us," Butch said as he reached out his hand to shake George's.